This
PJ BOOK
belongs to

PJ Library®

JEWISH BEDTIME STORIES and SONGS

Green Bean Books

First published in the UK in 2019
by Green Bean Books

c/o Pen & Sword Books Ltd
47 Church Street, Barnsley, S. Yorkshire, S70 2AS
www.greenbeanbooks.com

Hardback ISBN 978-1-78438-369-5
Paperback ISBN 978-1-78438-425-8

Designed by Tina Garcia
Edited by Claire Berliner, Julie Carpenter
and Kate Baker

Printed in China by 1010 Printing International Ltd

051929.6K1/B1402/A6

MIX
Paper from
responsible sources
FSC® C016973
FSC
www.fsc.org

THE SAGES OF CHELM AND THE MOON

Written by Shlomo Abas
Illustrated by Omer Hoffmann
Translated by Gilah Kahn-Hoffmann

Once upon a time in Eastern Europe, there was a small city called Chelm. The people there were known as "The Sages of Chelm" because they were supposedly very wise and intelligent. Many tales have been told about their deeds and adventures, but this is one of the most famous. It is the story of the people of Chelm and the moon...

On moonlit nights, when the sky was bright, the people of Chelm loved walking around. The streets, you see, were muddy, and there were no street lamps.

Only when the moon lit up
the darkness could they see
where they were going.

The darkest nights were those when the moon disappeared altogether
and barely a sliver of light could be seen in the sky. On such nights, the
poor people of Chelm bumped into each other, walked into tree trunks,
and stumbled over rocks in the road.

Sometimes they completely lost their way.
Some couldn't find their own homes and wandered
into their neighbours' houses by mistake!

Something had to be done, so the wise people of
Chelm held a meeting. They consulted, conferred, and
finally concluded that someone must be stealing the
moon from them. They made a decision that was,
of course, a very wise one.

They should buy a new moon. A trustworthy
moon. A moon that could not be taken away from
them. They asked all Chelmites to contribute to this
worthy cause. Before long, they had a healthy sum
of money – enough to buy a new moon.

On a dark, moonless night, a delegation
set off to search for a moon.

They travelled by horse and cart,
from town to town, climbing
mountains and crossing valleys.

For two weeks, they
travelled and searched,
searched and travelled.

Then, on the night of a full moon,
they reached an inn, where they
decided to spend the night.

"Where are you from?" the innkeeper asked the group.

"From Chelm," they said.

"And what is the purpose of your travels?"

"To buy something."

"What do you want to buy?"

"We're searching for a good moon. Our moon keeps disappearing. Someone is stealing it. Or maybe it's hiding on purpose to make us angry."

"Well," said the innkeeper. "I can sell you a wonderful moon. A moon that will always shine for you!"

"Great! How much do you want for it?"
asked the delegates.
"How much money do you have?" asked the
innkeeper. The wise Chelmites proudly revealed
the impressive sum that their community had
generously donated.

The innkeeper smiled to himself. "Well, it's not
really enough," he said slyly.
"But I know Chelm is not a rich city, so I will take it."

With that, the innkeeper filled a barrel with water and placed it outside, underneath the moon. He told the wise people of Chelm to look inside. They peered into the barrel and, sure enough, right there, glinting in the darkness, was the moon.

"What a radiant moon!" they cried in wonder and quickly handed their money to the innkeeper. The cunning innkeeper sealed the barrel, wrapped it in a huge sack, and tied it well. The Chelmites loaded it onto their cart and began the long journey home. But the barrel with the moon inside was heavy, and the horses were slow. And as the days passed, the moon, once again, disappeared from the sky.

The Chelmites passed through dark villages and towns, laughing and feeling smug. "For everyone else it's pitch black. Only in Chelm will the moon shine each and every night of the year!"

Finally, the delegates arrived home. As the sun set and darkness fell,
everyone in the city gathered in the square next to the synagogue
to see their new moon. The rabbi was invited to uncover the barrel.
He stepped forward and began to slowly untie the cord.

The Chelmites jostled with one another to see inside.
Gasps rippled through the crowd.

"There is no moon!" the people cried.
"We've been tricked!" exclaimed
the members of the delegation.
"That innkeeper must have stolen back
the moon when we weren't looking!"

The Sages of Chelm never did manage to buy themselves a moon. To this day, they enjoy radiant nights when the moon is in sight. And on nights when the moon can't be found, they fumble around in the darkness. Either way, the moon looks down on them and smiles – just as it does on us all.